Planet
Middle
School

Planet Middle School

NIKKI GRIMES

SCHOLASTIC INC.
New York Toronto London Auckland
Sydney Mexico City New Delhi Hong Kong

For my young friend and surrogate daughter,
Sheila Northcutt,
whose middle name should be Joy.

ISBN 978-0-545-43750-9

12 11 10 9 8 7 6   22/0

Printed in the U.S.A.   77

First Scholastic printing, January 2012

Book design by Yelena Safronova and Donna Mark

Heartsick

The emergency-room doors
crack open
and I feel my heart split.
The hospital smell
leaves me dizzy,
or maybe it's just my fear.
What if I got here too late?
What if my friend's eyes
never open?
What if I missed the chance
to say I'm sorry?
Our fights seem silly now.
But then,
so do the last few months.
I guess the joke is on me.
Too bad I don't feel
like laughing.

Names

Joylin was my mother's idea.
She says she swelled with joy
the moment she knew
I lay curled up
inside her.
While she waited
for my arrival,
she dreamed in pink,
imagined frilly dresses
and sweet tea parties.
Sorry, Mom.
Jockette is what
Caden calls me.
He's so lame.
If he weren't my brother,
I'd strangle him.
Just kidding.
So what's the big deal, anyway?
So I'm not a girly girl.
So what?
Is there some law?
I don't think so.

Tom Boy

What does that
even mean?
And where did it come from?
And if there's a Tom Boy,
how come there's no Jane Girl?
I'm just sayin'.

Basics

I go to my closet
grab a T-shirt and jeans.
Which pair will I wear?
Long jeans, cropped jeans,
just so they are baggy jeans.
Dad keeps asking Mom,
"Where's the girl
you promised me?"
Like he doesn't love
our games of one on one.
Please.

Sitting Pretty

Mom bugs me about
sitting with my legs
wide open.
But I don't get
what she's so worried about.
I'm covered up in blue jeans.
It's not like anyone
can see anything.
I've told her this
a million times.
For some reason,
she just keeps
shaking her head.

Signature

My friend KeeLee teases me
for always being dressed
head to toe
in navy.
I just roll my eyes
and tell her
it's my signature color.
She's just jealous
she doesn't have one.

Preacher's Kid

I.
KeeLee would swallow the rainbow
if she could.
She loves every single color.
"God made each one," says KeeLee.
"He doesn't pick favorites,
so why should I?"
KeeLee's a preacher's kid,
so she's got a different way
of looking at things.

II.
She chose me when we were nine.
At school, a bunch of girls
were making fun of me
for dressing like a boy.
I tried to act like I didn't care,
but KeeLee caught me balling my fists
and shoving them inside my pockets.
She pushed through the group
and came straight to my side.
"You're just jealous," she told those girls,
"'cause the boys don't want to play with *you*."
Then she slipped her arm through mine
and said, "Let's get out of here."

III.
KeeLee dresses frilly,
but she's tougher than me.
One day, a girl called her
Goody Two-shoes,
and KeeLee said,
"Well, you got the shoe part right!"
and walked away.
"You think being a Tom Boy is hard?
Try being a PK," says KeeLee.
"Everyone expects me to be perfect.
Like that's even possible."
KeeLee may not be an angel,
but she's practically perfect to me.

Conversation

Jake thinks KeeLee
is a little weird.
She was watching Jake and me
play ball one day
when he was off his game.
He kept putting "God"
and "damn" in the same sentence
every time he missed the hoop.
I cleared my throat
to get his attention,
nodded in KeeLee's direction
and whispered,
"Pastor's kid, remember?"
Jake turned red,
told KeeLee he was sorry.
"For what?" she asked.
"For taking God's name in vain."
"But you didn't," said KeeLee.
"Yes, I did."
"No, you didn't."
"Yes. I *did*."
"No," KeeLee said again.
"You didn't."
Jake looked too confused to spit

and I wasn't much better.
"My father says, God is who he is,
but that's not his name.
And you can't take his name in vain
if you don't even know what it is."
"So, what's his name, then?" asked Jake.
KeeLee smiled.
"I'm not telling.
If you want to know,
you'll have to ask him yourself."
Jake just shook his head
and threw his hands up.
I didn't know what to say,
but KeeLee's words
made me wonder
what other secrets
she and God shared.

Jake

Monday afternoon
I meet Jake for our weekly
game of one on one.
He takes the ball out
and I do my best to block him,
but he's too tall and solid
for me to break his play.
Didn't used to be that way.
Back in second grade
when we first met,
I was the one
with all the size.
Not sure when that changed.
But so what?
He's still one of my best friends,
him and KeeLee.
We play for an hour or so.
When it's time to find our way home,
he play-punches me
in the arm, like always,
only harder than I remember.
I must be getting soft.
"Later, dude," says Jake.
"Yeah, later," I say,
grinning through the pain.

Beginnings

I.
Jake moved to the neighborhood
right after his dad walked out
and left his mom a mess.
One December day, at recess
I found him all by himself,
clinging to a swing,
crying in the cold.
I plopped down on the swing
next to him,
pushed myself off the ground,
and kept him quiet company.
When I could see
he was done crying,
I said, "Hi. My name's Joy."
And he said, between sniffles,
"I'm Jake."
And that's all it took
to make us friends forever.

II.
When I had appendicitis
and thought I might die,
I woke up after surgery

and there was Jake
staring down at me,
saying "Hey!"
which was about
all the conversation
I was in the mood for.

III.
These days,
we're mostly basketball buddies.
Jake doesn't talk much,
but the silences between us
are filled with friendship.
I don't know what I'd do
without him.

New Math

Up till now,
the math of my life
has been pretty simple:
friends
plus family
plus sports.
What more
could I ask for, right?
But lately,
my outside has been changing
and my inside keeps telling me
more is on the way.
Trouble is,
I'm not sure
I'm ready.

Ridges

Ridges, that's all they are.
Two weird mounds ruining
the perfect flatness
of my chest.
I do the best I can
to hide them,
wearing too-tight undershirts
stolen from
my baby brother's dresser.
(Okay, so Caden's not technically a baby,
but he's two years younger than me,
so that qualifies.)
God, forgive me, but
I need those shirts.
I just can't have
those things on my chest
bouncing around
every time I charge down
the basketball court.
I want all eyes
on the swish
as my perfect layup shot
clears the net.

The Usual

The minute Dad walks in the door
he starts grilling me:
"So?
How did the basketball tryouts go?
What did the coach say?"
I bite back a smile
and pretend annoyance.
"What about it, sport?
Did you make the team?"
"Probably," I hedge,
wanting to watch
his excitement build.
Dad pats me on the back.
"Okay. It's your decision.
I think you'd be good, though."
He falls silent
and my brother, Caden,
steps in the gap.
"Hey, Dad.
Look at this!"
He holds up his drawing
of a pitcher on the mound.
"My teacher says
it's one of the best drawings
she's ever seen."

"That's nice," Dad whispers
and turns away,
letting all the air
out of Caden's balloon
and mine.

B-Day

Back from a killer game
at the neighborhood b-ball court,
I dribble through the living room
like I don't know better
till Mom tells me to stop,
then I cut to the kitchen
where water waits.
I'm two glasses down
and working on a third
when Mom makes me
sputter up water
like a busted faucet.
"That's it," she says.
"No more training bras.
Time to take you shopping
for the real thing."
Where is a parallel universe
when you need one?

Humiliation

"No, Mom.
You cannot come into
the dressing room with me!"
I face the torture
on my own,
fumble with assorted A cups,
plain and padded,
turn myself into a human pretzel
trying to fasten the stupid little hooks
across my back.
I'm sure there's some
trick to it.
Then finally, I'm in,
locked down,
nothing moving,
feeling like I've just
been sentenced
to jail.

Planet Middle School

"It was embarrassing,"
I told KeeLee.
"I'm trying on all these
strange contraptions,
and my mom's right outside
the dressing room,
dying for a peek!"
KeeLee shrugged.
"You're growing up," she said.
"That always weirds out parents."
"Still."
"I know."
Thank God for KeeLee.
She's the only familiar thing
about this crazy school year.
Bad enough my body's
turned against me.
On top of that
everything else is new:
new school, new teacher,
new classrooms
I need a map to find.
I swear, some days
I feel like an alien,

dropped off on
Planet Middle School
by mistake.
I keep scanning the skies,
searching for that spaceship
that's gonna take me home.

Last Straw

Over dinner,
Mom and Dad
slip into their usual ritual
discussing the day
and Mom casually mentions
"Joy and I went
bra shopping."
I grab a napkin
to cough into
and slide down
in my seat.
"Good," says my bratty brother.
"Maybe now she'll stop
stealing my undershirts."
That does it.
I bolt from the table
and make my getaway.
I've had more than enough
embarrassment
for one day.

Hunger Pangs

Three hours later,
I'm still chasing sleep.
My stomach growls at me
as if I'm the one to blame
for skipping dinner.
It's all Mom's fault, and Caden's!
I complain into my pillow,
which gets me nowhere
so I sneak into the kitchen
for a late-night snack.

Early Warning Signs

Don't ask me
what's up with KeeLee
all of a sudden.
I haven't got a clue.
Today we're walking
to Spanish,
and she puts a finger
to her lips,
warning me to shush.
Next thing I know,
John Taylor passes by
(He's in the *ninth grade!*)
flaming red hair
bouncing off his shoulders.
KeeLee flips his curls
quick, so he won't notice,
then bites her lip
to keep from laughing
out loud.
What is *with* her?
"You never used to care about
some boy's stupid hair," I tell her.
"Whatever," she says.

"People change."
I shake my head, thinking,
Not me.

Oh, Joy

End of the day,
I lay my head
on my desk,
faking the migraine
I'm certain
is on its way.
Imaginary numbers?
Come on!
Who dreams up this stuff?
It's enough to make
anybody ill.
I practically scream for joy
when the bell rings.

Artiste

Homework done
I run out for some air,
handball resting in my palm.
I slam the thing
against the brownstone wall
while Caden studies me
through the window the way
he sometimes does,
his hand a busy bird
flying across a page
of his drawing pad.
Back inside,
I breathe heavy over
Caden's shoulder.
The action pose he's drawn of me
nearly leaps in the air.
I tell him so
and watch my words
paint a smile on his face.
Then I go and spoil it.
"You should show that to Dad."
Caden stares at me
like I've grown two heads
and I can't blame him.

"Well, show it to Mom, anyway."
He nods and I leave the room
before I manage to say
something else stupid.

Worthless

It's a wonder
my brother hasn't completely given up
on showing Dad his drawings.
One time, all Caden got was
"Too bad you can't
go out for a sport
like your sister,
instead of wasting your time
doodling."
Ouch.

Through the Walls

It's not often
Mom raises her voice,
but that night,
her words beat their way
through the bedroom wall.
"If you're not careful with Caden,
you're going to lose that boy!"
she tells my dad.
"And you won't have
anyone to blame
but yourself."
All I hear from Dad
is a grunt.
I burrow deeper
under my covers
praying that Caden
is already asleep.

Game On

The very next day, Caden
begs me for basketball lessons,
just him and me.
He says he'd be too embarrassed
around Jake
or other guys.
Anyway, all he wants,
he says,
is a few tips on
how to make the backboard squeal,
how to make Dad take notice.

Busy

The next days bounce by
fast as God can dribble them.
I race to keep up:
Caden's lessons, games with Jake,
visits with KeeLee—and school!

Cravings

I wake up in the middle of the night
crazy for a piece of chocolate
as if my life depends on it.
I feel under my pillow
like there's some secret stash
I should know about,
then roll over
and finally go back to sleep.

It's Official

First thing in the morning,
stomach pains send me
to the bathroom
where I discover
that some things change inside you
whether you want them to
or not.

Period

That's a good name for it.
It's the end of life
as I know it.

The Curse

I lie in bed
curled in a ball tight enough
to stuff through a hoop.
"No playing for me today,"
I whisper to Michael Jordan
staring at me from a poster
on my wall.
Another colossal cramp
shoots through me
and I'm thinking:
Boys have it easy.

Lunch Line

Feeling better,
it's back to school.
The morning flies by
and soon, it's time for lunch.
The line goes on forever.
"Hey, Joy."
It's KeeLee, three inches taller
than yesterday.
"Heels, KeeLee?"
I know my friend's
in there somewhere
behind the lip gloss
and wanna-be stilettos.
KeeLee shrugs.
"I just thought I'd give them a try.
I'll probably go back to flats tomorrow."
I decide to study shoes,
see how many other
three-inch heels I can count.
One. Two. Five.
Without planning to,
I find my eyes traveling
up a pair of calves
attached to a cute boy with

chocolate brown skin
in shorts and a tight tee
clinging to—
"Quit it!" I tell myself.
My stomach growls
loud enough for others to hear
and for once, I don't care.
The distraction is exactly
what I need.

Text

A handful of words
shot into cyberspace
explode into smiles:
"KeeLee, I made the team!"
"Joy, I made the choir!"

Bragging

Dad claps Caden
on the back.
An Etch A Sketch
of momentary joy
spreads across his face.
My brother's too happy
to calculate
the why of Dad's attention.
"Did you hear
the good news, son?"
asks Dad.
"Your sister here made the team!"
And just like that
my brother's smile
disappears.

The Evil Eye

I bite my lip
to keep from telling Dad
he's clueless.
Instead, I grab Caden's hand
and drag him to the kitchen
to help me set the table,
anything to distract him
for a minute.
But I throw Dad
the dirtiest look
I can manage.
It's what Mom calls
the Evil Eye.

The Produce Section

Sometimes I feel
like slave labor
forced to run errands
whenever my mother gets a whim.
"Say!" says Mom. "I think I'll make
buckwheat pancakes with bananas.
Doesn't that sound great?
We're a little low on syrup though,
and I could use an extra banana.
Joylin?"
Next thing I know,
I'm slouching down
a supermarket aisle
like I got nothing better to do.
I growl at the list
that grew to ten items
by the time I hit the door.
I'm grumbling about
the unfairness of life
when this cute guy reaches around me
and grabs a plum tomato.
"Excuse me," he says
as if he needs to apologize
for being fine

and popping into my life
long enough for me to get close
to his sweet-smelling beautifulness.
He continues down the aisle
I just left behind
and my head swivels
so I can go on staring.
There I am, grinning, when *bang*—
I crash my cart into
this nice old lady
since I wasn't watching
where I was going.
"Sorry. Sorry," I say
turning three shades of purple.
I close my eyes and count to ten.
"Okay," I say to myself.
"What am I looking for again?
Oh, yeah.
Bananas."

It's Not My Fault

There are suddenly
cute boys everywhere,
I swear.
They keep popping up
all the time.

Not My Kind of Exercise

My English teacher
is out to ruin my day.
"I want each of you
to write a poem
about a topic
that interests you," she says.
Don't get me wrong.
I love to write, but I hate
these on-the-spot assignments.
My brain always freezes.
I study the clock,
count down
the remaining minutes
of this torture
and scribble something about
running against the wind.

Bell

The bell rings at last.
I spring from my seat and dash
to the locker room.

Locker Room

They call her Glory,
the girl who has the locker
next to mine.
She's the same age as me,
only more like—
I don't know—
a lady.
Her silver hoop earrings,
armload of bangles,
and painted fingernails
tell me she's
nothing to worry about—
some girly girl who probably
shouldn't even have made the team.
I'm sure I'm right
till we hit the gym
and she dribbles the ball so fast
all you see
is a blur.
Guess I counted her out
too soon.

Lunchroom

Glory spots me
in the lunchroom,
waves me over to the table
with a bunch of other
girls from the team.
I'm so used to
playing with the boys,
it's strange to be with girls
who play the game
as hard as me.
I join them,
trying not to stare
at the perfection
of Glory's hair,
a cascade of braids
framing her face.
Here she is in her
lace-trimmed tee,
this serious jock
who looks nothing
like me.

Silent Shift

On the way out,
I pass by KeeLee
laughing with her new friends
from show choir.
We smile and wave
at each other
like our not sitting together
is no big deal.

History

KeeLee texts me
in the middle of history.
Good thing the teacher
doesn't catch me
with the phone in my hand.
What excuse could I use?
I'm exploring the history
of technology?
"Come over for dinner,"
she texts.
"Can't," I answer.
"My mom has
an exciting evening
planned for me."
"Got it," types KeeLee.
"Laundry."
That girl knows me
too well.

Risky Business

Nobody told me
the Laundromat could be
a danger zone.
There I am
minding my own business
studying the slow turn of the dryer
when here comes
this six-foot-tall
chocolate chip,
muscles rippling like Denzel
in *The Hurricane*,
and suddenly I'm imagining
my hand swallowed up in his
my head nuzzling his shoulder
my—
the ear-splitting dryer buzzer
brings me back to reality
and I make myself busy
folding sheets.

Butterfingers

Give me an "F" for frustration
and you can spell out
the next afternoon.
That's when Caden's on the court.
I call him to the throw line,
grab his hand, and press
our palms together
to measure size.
His hand is already
larger than mine.
So why can't he keep the ball
from slipping away
in the middle of a dribble?
It's a mystery to me,
but he keeps saying
"Wait! Wait!
Let me try again."
Mom says
that's one thing her kids
have in common:
We're both
stubborn as sin.

Teacher

KeeLee and I
follow our gym class
out into the school courtyard
for a jog.
The new phys-ed teacher
runs back and forth alongside us
to keep an eye on everyone's pace.
KeeLee can't take her eyes
off of him.
"What exactly are you staring at?" I ask.
"You gotta be kidding!
Don't tell me you missed
that bodacious butt."
"KeeLee!"
"What?" KeeLee looks all innocent.
"Bodacious isn't a bad word."
I lower my gaze
and check out the teacher's
southern hemisphere,
and a minute later,
I'm giggling like
every teenage girl
I've ever made fun of.
I bite my tongue

to stifle my silliness,
but it doesn't help.
I'm already
too far gone.

Girls Will Be Boys

On Saturday,
I try to shake off whatever this weird
giggly-thing is
that's happening to me.
I hit the local basketball court,
make the boys groan, like always,
butting into their game,
stealing the ball
like I belong there.
What're they gonna do,
hit a girl?
So they put up with me.
I charge downcourt
ready to slam past
the guard shadowing me
a little too closely
for my use.
Who is this guy?
I look up past the knees,
catch sight of sweet brown curls
bouncing above killer green eyes
rimmed with the longest lashes
I've ever seen,
and I lose it.

The ball is gone
before I know it,
and I'm shaking my head.
What's the matter with me?
How could I let
some boy get me
off my game?

After

Far as I'm concerned,
the game is over.
I excuse myself
and limp off the court,
pretending a pulled hamstring.
The only thing worse
than losing my game
is Jake catching me.
"Why was you staring down Santiago?"
is the way he puts it.
"It's *were* staring down, Jake,
and I wasn't staring down anybody."
"So you say."
I'm pretty sure
that's a smirk
Jake is wearing on his face,
and I'm not having it.
"Good-bye, Jake," I say,
happy nobody can tell
when I blush.
Plus, I get one good thing
for my embarrassment.
I find out the new boy's name
is Santiago.

Santiago

Turns out,
he's not new
to the neighborhood.
So how come
I never noticed him
before?

Dinner Chatter

"Hey, bud,"
Dad says,
"Jake told me
he saw you down
at the basketball court last week."
"Yeah," says Caden,
grin splitting his face in two.
"Good for you!" says Dad.
Caden passes me
a look that says,
"See? It's already working!
Dad's starting to notice me."
I'm thinking,
Yeah, but wait
till he sees you
try to play.

Speechless

I'm losing my mind,
I'm sure of it.
Yesterday, that cute boy
Santiago said hello
and I completely lost
my power of speech.
I mean, I opened my mouth
and out came . . .
nothing at all.
What's wrong with me?

Boy Watch

I can't help it.
I start watching Santiago
watching girls in the hall.
How dumb is that?
I try to talk myself
out of my stupidity,
but then I notice
every one of them
wears makeup
and tight shirts
and short skirts.
My naked lips
form the words:
"Guess that leaves me out."

The Closet

I search my closet for
a single outfit that would qualify
as pretty.
Of course, I come up empty.
"Pretty" has never been
part of my vocabulary.
But that was pre-Santiago.
Is that my phone?
I let the call go
to voicemail.
I'm not leaving this closet
till I find something
semi-pretty
to wear.

Message

Oh, no!
It was Jake's call
I missed
on purpose.
We were supposed to meet.
How could I forget?

Apology

"Sorry I didn't show up,"
I tell Jake
when I call that evening.
"Where were you?" he asks.
"I waited for almost an hour!"
"Sorry," I repeat,
stalling until I can figure out
what to say.
I'm usually honest with Jake,
but this truth is just too lame.
"I was studying for a test," I tell him.
"I guess I lost track of time."
I'm holding my breath
but don't even know it
until I hear him say,
"Yeah, well, don't do it again."

Unspoken

Back from another practice,
Caden and I find Mom
in the living room
thumbing through one of his
old drawing pads,
her crescent moon smile
lighting up her eyes.
"Hey! Where'd you find that?"
asks Caden,
snatching the pad
from Mom's fingers.
"I thought it was lost."
"I found it under the coffee table,"
she says.
"Bottom shelf.
Must've moved it there one day
when I was cleaning.
Which reminds me," says Mom,
"I haven't seen you
drawing in a while.
Why is that?"
Caden shrugs,
all the answer
he plans on giving.

To Be Honest

Secretly,
I'm with Mom on this.
I miss Caden's drawings.
I hate to see him give up
something he's so good at
just to try to be
like me.

Lipstick

I stand in front of
Mom's vanity
like most girls do at three,
splashing on perfume
and smearing blush
from cheek to ear.
And here I am,
snagging lipstick.
"Crimson Touch"
is a nice name.
I wipe it across my lips,
then dash out the door
before Mom can catch me.
Minutes later, I meet up with KeeLee
and we strut through the school hall,
me waiting for my chance
to impress Him.
I'm all smiles when I see Santiago,
which is when KeeLee starts
poking me. But I ignore her
'cause all I can think about
is Santiago, who
takes one look at me
and laughs out loud.

Not the reaction
I was hoping for.
KeeLee pokes me again.
"You've got lipstick
on your teeth, silly.
I tried to tell you."
My hand flies to my mouth
too late.
I sprint to the girl's room,
leave "Crimson Touch"
on wads of toilet paper,
suddenly realizing the color
looks just like blood.
Disgusting.
Can this day
get any worse?

Busted

Of course
the first person
I run into on my block
is Jake.
"Dude! Your lip is bleeding.
No, wait.
It's your whole mouth!"
The lipstick must have left
a stain on my lips.
I sigh and roll my eyes,
in no mood to explain.
"Hey, Jake.
What's up?"
"You tell *me*," he says
studying my lips.
"It's lipstick," I mumble.
Jake laughs.
"You gotta be kidding!"
I burn him with a stare.
"Sorry," he says.
"I didn't know
you were into that
sort of thing."
I shrug.

"Just thought I'd give it a try."
"O-*kay*," says Jake.
"But why?"
"None of your business!" I say,
wanting to get off of the subject.
"Dang! Somebody's in
a rotten mood today.
Later," he says,
and jogs off
before I tell him
to leave me alone.

Help

I need help with this makeup stuff.
KeeLee doesn't know
much more than me.
Too bad I'm not
Cinderella.
A fairy godmother
would come in handy
right about now.

Advice

I slip out of my
sweaty gym clothes
and hit the showers.
Toweled off and half dressed,
I find my voice
before Glory has a chance
to leave.
"I like your makeup," I say,
feeling silly.
"I mean, the colors are nice."
"Thanks," she says.
"I wish—"
My tongue stumbles.
"There's this boy—
I mean—"
Why is my mouth
suddenly useless?
"I try to get him
to look at me, but—"
Thank God,
Glory steps in.
"You want a makeup tip?"
I nod. That seems safer
than speech.

"Keep it simple.
A little blush,
a little lip gloss.
That's it. Okay?"
I nod again,
smiling, relieved.
Still feeling ridiculous, though,
but at least
Glory didn't laugh.

Practice Does Not Make Perfect

Today
it's layup shots
for Caden.
Of course,
he stinks at this.
One of these days,
I'm going to have to tell him so.
I just don't know how.

Useful Noise

Back home,
I sprint ahead,
take two stairs
at a time,
duck into the bathroom
and lock the door.
Just before I switch on
the shower,
Caden yells,
"Hey! How did I do today?"
I turn the water on
full blast.
"Sorry!" I yell back.
"I can't hear you!"

Hair

I step from the shower,
catch sight of my wild mane
in the mirror.
Something makes me pause,
capture a damp curl in my fingers,
and pull.
Wonder what I'd look like
if I gave up my usual ponytail
for braids?

Scar

Some monstrous thing
crawled under my skin last night
while I was sleeping,
something hideous that left
a bulging bump on the middle
of my cheek.
This thing's the size
of Kilimanjaro,
so it's not like
I can hide it.
With my luck,
Santiago will notice me today,
and how exactly
am I supposed to
explain this thing away?

Enough

Today,
I push Caden into a game
with the neighborhood boys
so he can see
just how bad he is.
A half hour in
he's swimming in sweat
from chasing up and down the court,
bruised from one too many
body blows
from playing guard,
mad from losing his grip
on the ball
each time he manages
to get his hand on it
for a second.
I shake my head
and yell, "Time!"
then pull him aside.
Give it up
is what I'm thinking.
Instead, I say,
"Go home, Caden.
Just—go home."

He clenches his fist,
glares at me,
and stomps off the court.

The Plan

The next day,
Caden shows up at my door,
stares silently for the longest.
"What?" I finally ask.
"I thought you got it, Joy.
I thought you understood
why I need to learn that game."
I sigh, set aside
Bridge to Terabithia,
and tell my little brother
what he doesn't want to hear.
"You're okay at sports, Caden,
but your heart's just not in it
and that shows."
Now it's Caden's turn to sigh.
"I know. I just thought—
since Dad—
you know."
We both sit silent
till an idea comes to me.
"Hey! Dad's birthday
is coming up soon.
Why not do a drawing for him?
You're so good at that," I say.

Caden rolls his eyes.
"No, seriously.
Do a portrait of him.
He'll really look at it this time.
Trust me. He doesn't want
to make Mom mad."
"Maybe," says Caden.
"I bet he'll love it.
You could even do it from
one of his favorite photos.
Like that old one
when he was captain
of his basketball team."
I can see Caden's wheels
start to turn.
"You think so?"
I don't answer.
I just smile.

Seven Kinds of Sorry

The next game
of one on one with Jake
is not what it used to be,
not half as rough
or wordless.
It's got a new vocabulary
with seven kinds of sorry.
Jake says it every time
he knocks into me on the court
or grazes my leg
or if our chests bump
when we both jump
for the hoop,
him trying to score,
me trying to steal the ball,
or vice versa.
Sorry.
Sorry.
Sorry!
I wish he'd come up
with some other way to say
I didn't mean
to touch you that way.

I wish he'd quit
saying it
at all.

Looking Back

I sit in my room
at my desk
flipping the wings
of one of the model airplanes
Jake and I
used to build together.
So what if I was a girl,
he was a boy?
Life was simple then.
There was no weirdness.
We were just—friends.

I'm Texting as Fast as I Can

"I'm missing U, KeeLee."

"Me 2 U."

"Coming to the girls game today?
We're playing Woodruff MS."

"Can't. Choir."

"Bummer."

"I know."

This is a new dance
for KeeLee and me.
We still haven't learned
all the steps.

Woodruff Never Had a Chance

Thirty seconds on the clock,
I block out screams
from the bleachers,
power downcourt,
get in place for a pass
from Glory.
Ball in hand,
I feint left,
feint right,
push forward,
work the poor girl
guarding me
into a lather,
then fly for the net
and *swoosh!*
I'm so hot
it hurts!
If only Santiago
could see me.

Kudos

I feel a pat
on the back,
turn and find Jake
grinning enough
for the both of us.
"Not bad, kid," he says.
"Glad to see
you remember everything
I taught you."
I give him
a little shove.
"You wish!" I say.
"Why didn't you tell me
you were coming?"
"There's this thing
called a surprise.
Have you heard of it?"
That earns Jake
an eye roll,
but he just ignores it.
"I don't see any
earrings or lipstick.
That must mean
you're not expecting

Santiago."
I shoot Jake a look
that shuts him up.
He raises his hands in surrender.
"See you later," says Jake.
All he gets from me
is a nod.

Obsessed

I spend the morning
noticing hair:
straight, curly,
wavy, dreads,
braids, twists.
It's like I'm shopping
for the style that's right
for me.
Then later, I see Santiago,
whose brown curls are
too beautiful for words.
In the packed cafeteria,
I sneak up behind him,
stroke his hair,
and race past him so fast
I crash into a support beam
I never even noticed was there.
That was hours ago
and the roomful of laughter
is still ringing in my ears.

Reminiscing

Don't know what makes parents
decide to reminisce,
but tonight Mom turns up
in my doorway
in the mood.
"When I was a girl,
I loved to climb trees," she says.
I look out at the lifeless
lampposts that fill
our street, our city,
and wonder *where*.
"Then one day," Mom drones on,
"I just didn't feel like
scrambling up trees anymore,
and it was okay,
you know?"
I nod, thinking,
There's got to be a point
in there somewhere.
I just can't figure out
what.

The Hang-Up

All evening
I think about calling Jake,
about telling him what happened
with me crashing into
that support beam.
It's the sort of thing
we used to laugh about.
Only this time
the girl in the story
is me.
I pick up the phone,
then put it down again.
I love my friend, but
the last thing I need
is to mention anything
that has to do with Santiago.
Jake doesn't need to know
what kind of crazy girl
that boy has turned me into.

Huddle

I don't like the strangeness
between Jake and me lately,
so when Mom mentions
he hasn't been over for dinner
in a while
I invite him.
Everything seems normal again,
him kicking me under the table,
chewing with his mouth wide open
so only I can see,
both of us sticking our tongues out
at our plates
like we did when we were eight.
Later, washing dishes,
I ask why he's the same old Jake
when he comes over for dinner
but all weird
when we play basketball these days.
He shrugs. "That's different," he says.
"Why?"
"Because, you know. *You* are."
I argue.
"I'm the same me
I've always been."

"No," says Jake, shaking his head.
"Now, you're—"
"A girl?" I finish for him.
"Exactly!" he says.
"Big whoop!
I've always been a girl, Jake."
"I know," he says. "But now
you look like one."
I drop a dish back in the sink,
send bubbles flying.
"Yeah, well," I tell Jake,
 "get over it!"

Just Like Old Times

The old Caden is back,
him with his nose in a book
or sketching every time
I turn around,
while I'm busy
slamming the backboards.
One Saturday, Dad says,
"It's a beautiful day out there, son,"
like Caden can't see that.
"Don't you want to go play ball?"
Caden shakes his head,
carefully shading
the face he's just drawn.
"No thanks," he tells Dad,
who immediately
starts to frown.
"Joylin plays enough
for the both of us."

Lonely Lobes

One morning
I wash my face
then study my reflection
trying to figure out
what's missing.
I pull my hair back
and there's the answer.
I run to my parents' room,
bang on the door, and yell,
"Mom! I need to get
my ears pierced!"
I hear her whisper,
"Finally!"

Pierced

My new twelve-carat
gold studs gleam
even in the fake glow
of the lunchroom lights.
They sparkle and scream
"Look at me! Look at me!"
At least, they'd better
since every time
I turn those stupid things
to help keep the holes open
until they completely heal,
I feel the burn.

Studs

I jog onto the court
dribble back and forth
to warm up while I wait for Jake.
He sneaks up behind me
and steals the ball.
He's all ready to play
till he looks at me
and catches a flash of gold.
"Earrings, Joy?
You're wearing earrings now?"
"So?"
"You never wear earrings," says Jake.
"It's no big deal," I say.
Jake palms the ball and stares at me.
"I know why you're doing this," he says.
"Doing what?"
"The earrings, the hair, the lipstick.
It's all about Santiago."
"I don't know
what you're talking about."
I can play dumb
with the best of them.
"I see the way you act
when he's around," says Jake.

"You suddenly start
messing with your hair
and pulling on your clothes
to make sure they're straight."
Jake doesn't usually talk much,
so when he does, his words hang heavy.
I jog in place, impatient
to change the subject.
Truth or consequences
is not my game.
Besides, I can't talk to Jake
about Santiago.
He'd only laugh.
I smack the ball out of Jake's hand.
"Are we gonna play or not?"
Jake shakes his head,
snatches the ball,
and drives it to the hoop.
It's all ball and no talk after that,
which suits me just fine.

Doubt

Time for school photos again.
I clutter my bed
with outfit rejects
and turn to KeeLee for
a little assistance.
"Who *are* you?" she asks me.
"And what have you done
with my friend?"
"What do you mean?"
KeeLee sighs.
"You used to know exactly
what you wanted
      to wear
      to do
      to listen to.
But these days,
you can't even choose
what to eat for lunch."
I shrug, like it's no biggie,
except she's right.
At least, I think she is.
Or maybe not.
I can't decide.

School Photos

Flash those pearly whites.
Pretend you're a movie star
except for the zit.

It's Not What You Think

Mom comes in from work,
catches me watching
Sex and the City again.
She snatches the remote
and switches the screen to black
before I can blink.
"You've got no business
watching that show," she says.
"I've told you that once before.
What do you find so fascinating
about that show, anyway?"
I keep the answer to myself
so she won't laugh.
She'd never guess
that it's all about the shoes.
I keep wondering
how those girls
manage to walk
in those shoes,
and how on earth
will I ever learn?

Behind Closed Doors

I shuffle into the kitchen
one morning
and catch Caden
bent over his drawing pad.
Hearing me,
he slams the thing shut
(think diary,
minus the lock and key).
"Is that Dad's portrait?"
I ask.
"Quiet!" Caden orders.
"Or you'll spoil the surprise!"
I back off, hands in the air
showing surrender,
but I've got to laugh.
I could say
"Hey! It was my idea
in the first place."
But I don't
because that would be
immature.

Homework

I.
Doing homework at KeeLee's
can be lonely.
She's faster than me
and usually gets bored
waiting for me to finish
so we can just hang out.
She says she doesn't mind, though,
especially since we don't
get to see each other as much
as we used to.
Today when she's done
she jets to the kitchen
for a snack.
A few minutes later,
I decide to take a break
and join her,
my mouth watering
at the thought of chips.
But I guess
they'll have to wait.
KeeLee's been busy
painting her nails.
She blows on them,

then flashes her fingers
in my face.
"You like?" she asks.
I nod, then stare down
at my own nails,
jagged and dirty.
Not pretty like KeeLee's or Glory's.
Not the kind of nails
a certain boy would notice.
Before I can think about it too long,
I hold my hands out toward KeeLee
and say,
"Do mine!"

II.
KeeLee lets me sort through
her stash of nail polish colors.
One is called "Iridescent Black."
"You're kidding me!" I say
"What?" asks KeeLee.
"Your dad lets you wear this?"
"Why wouldn't he?"
"Well, I just thought—"
"Let me guess: You just thought
a pastor's kid
can't wear black nail polish.

Or say 'butt.' Or wear heels.
I get it," snaps KeeLee.
I whisper, "Sorry,"
then wait
for Hurricane KeeLee
to pass.

III.
KeeLee sets out
the base coat and polish,
giving herself a minute
to calm down.
She opens the first bottle,
grabs my left hand,
and works in silence.
One coat is finished
before she speaks again.
"Sorry," she says.
"It's just hard sometimes
fighting to be myself.
I get so tired of people
putting me in a box
'cause I'm a pastor's kid.
And the thing is,
God doesn't even care
about stuff like

what color nail polish I wear,
and neither does my dad.
He cares about *me*,
what kind of person I am inside."
Nails still wet,
I risk giving KeeLee
a monster hug.
"I know what kind of person you are,"
I tell her.
"The best."

Quick Question

I'm losing a game to Jake,
his five shots
to my two.
Out of the blue,
he asks,
"You and KeeLee
ever talk about me?"
"Why?"
"Just wondered,"
says Jake,
stealing the ball
while I'm distracted.
I ignore his casual tone.
If he's got KeeLee
on the brain,
there's more than wondering
going on.
I let it go,
for now.

Practice

The house quiet,
I leave my door open
certain I'm alone.
I walk back and forth
across my room,
flashing my shiny blue nails,
trying to swish my hips
like I've seen other girls do.
I'm pretty sure I've got it,
but I decide to try one more time
for good measure,
which is right about when
I catch sight of Caden's reflection
in my mirror.
He's standing in the hall,
grinning,
shaking his head.
I slam the door shut wondering
how long it would take
my parents to notice
if I just accidentally
shoved my brother
over a cliff.

Birthday Dinner

Birthday cake ablaze,
Dad blows out the candles
keeping the wish to himself
if he made one.
Caden's wish is no secret.
He slides his thin present
across the table and waits,
jaws clenched so tight
I hear them squeak.
I whisper a prayer for him
then say, "Come on, Dad!
Open it already!"
He finally frees a frame
from the wrapping
and stares down
at his portrait.
The surprise and wonder
that dance in his eyes
is a picture all its own.
He looks up at Caden
in the hush that follows.
"Son, you did this?"
he asks.
Caden swallows,

shakes his head
and I realize
I'm holding my breath.
"This is amazing, Caden,"
says Dad.
"Thank you."
Next thing I know,
I'm on my feet and clapping
while my pesky little brother
takes a bow.

Better Than Cake

Dad cuts his cake,
gives the first piece to Caden.
A pair of Cheshire cats,
neither of them
can stop grinning.
"Son, you may not be able
to play basketball
like your sister,
but you've got a gift
of your own."
Where are my sunglasses?
My brother's smile
is blinding.

Told You So

"See what happens
when you stop trying to be
someone you're not,
when you stick with
who you really are?
Good things follow."
I'm in my stride now,
wagging a wise finger
in my brother's face.
"I know," says Caden.
"You keep telling me.
Now quit it."

Heels

Next morning,
I'm having second thoughts.
The heels I borrowed from Mom
are pretty, though.
Strawberry to match
my lip gloss,
my patent-leather pointed toes
peek from beneath
my cuffed blue jeans.
I slip them on just before
I leave the house
so Mom won't have time
to make a fuss.
It's bad enough
Caden catches me
and laughs.
At school,
I tiptoe down the hall,
now and then touching the wall
for support.
My pinched toes
make me want to scream
till Santiago
comes onto the scene.

Then I'm all smiles.
Too bad that's not
the last thing I remember.
A second later,
my ankle gives way
and I'm on the floor,
Santiago holding out a hand
to help me up,
which means
I got half of what
I wanted:
I made an impression
on Santiago.
Just not
the right one.

Run

After school,
Jake calls
asking me to meet him
for a run.
I rub my sore ankle
and wince.
"No running for me today,"
I say.
I just don't tell him
why.

Daydreaming

I walk into a room
and Santiago breezes by everyone
who stands between us.
He reaches me
and stares down into my eyes
like no one else
is there.
He cups my face
in his strong hands,
leans in close,
and our lips—
"Joylin!" says the teacher.
"Please tell the class
the answer to the question."
"What?"

Movie Night

Movie night,
our code words for
hanging out.
KeeLee comes
for dinner
so we have time
to catch up.
Jake pops in later.
"Hey, Joy," he says,
then switches voices.
"Hello, KeeLee."
"Hey, Jake," she says,
then looks back
at the television.
I give Jake
a sharp look,
see his eyes
full of KeeLee,
and pull him down
on the couch right
next to me.
"Let's watch a movie,"
I say, not bothering
to take a vote.

I start the movie
and dim the lights.
I am *not* having one of my friends
make googly eyes
at the other.
Forget it.

The Day After

KeeLee and I
find our old table
in the lunchroom,
leaving show choir
and the girls from my team
on their own.
"That was weird last night,"
says KeeLee.
"What?"
"You know.
Jake kept staring at me like
I don't know."
She looks down at her plate.
"Like pizza.
With extra cheese."
"Oh. That," I say.
Should I tell her?
I wonder.
"A while back, he asked me
if we ever
talk about him."
"When?"
"I don't know.
A few weeks ago," I say.

"I think—he likes you."
There. I said it.
"Really?"
I hate the way she says it,
twirling a braid
around her finger.
"He *is* kind of cute," she says.
"KeeLee!"
Then she bursts out laughing.
"I'm just kidding, Joylin.
You should see your face!
Look, Jake's your friend
and me messing around with him
would just be too—icky.
So forget it, okay?"
I breathe again
relieved that I'm not going
to lose one friend
to another.

Skirting the Issue

I charge through the doors
of a discount clothing store
on the hunt for a bargain.
The few dollars I earn doing chores
will only go so far.
I journey down the skirt aisle,
an explorer in unfamiliar territory,
tossing semi-cute selections
into my basket
as I go.
Once in the dressing room,
I take turns pulling
each skirt on,
then spin before
the mirror thinking:
One of these
is bound to catch
Santiago's eye.

Caught

One morning finds me
in the kitchen
popping a frozen waffle
into the toaster,
trying to scarf it down
before anyone comes in.
"Morning, Joy," says Mom.
Too late.
"Hi, Mom. Bye, Mom."
I break for the door.
"Wait a minute," she says.
"What is that you've got on?"
"They're called clothes, Mom."
She gives me that look that says
I'm going to smack you
in a minute.
I hang my head,
pinching myself for being
such a smart mouth.
"Sorry," I mutter,
and take another step.
"You're wearing a skirt," she says,
like I don't know.
"Yes."

"You don't own a skirt."
"I do now. Bought it yesterday."
"You bought it?"
"Yes."
"With your own money?"
"*Yes.*"
By now, I'm bouncing
from foot to foot,
itching to be anywhere
but here.
A slow smile spreads
across my mom's face
like sun rising.
"Okay, baby," she says,
ready to let me go.
"You have a good day."
I breathe,
and smile back thinking,
That's the plan.

Runway

Walking to school,
an arctic blast
blows up my skirt
and I shiver,
wishing for the warmth
of jeans.
But I'm on a mission
so I spend the day
sitting cross-legged
pretending to be comfortable.
(If only Mom could see me!)
At lunch, I keep an eye out
for Santiago.
I spot him on the way
back to class,
and saunter by slow enough
so he'll notice.
Instead, he barely nods.
Embarrassed, I try
to tear up the nearest stairs
two at a time, like always,
only my too-cute pencil skirt
makes that impossible.
My quick getaway

is further interrupted
when I trip and my books
go flying across the stairs.
I bend to gather them
and hear kids giggling
as they stare at my thighs.
I stand up quickly,
cursing the skirt,
wishing for an invisibility cloak,
wondering if Santiago
is worth all this trouble
in the first place.

I Don't Get It

I thought I had him figured out,
the kind of hair he likes,
the clothes,
the shoes,
the makeup.
Why won't he even
notice me?
Where did I go wrong?

Fire Drill

"Joy," KeeLee whispers,
standing next to me
as we line up,
"since when did you
like wearing skirts?"
"Since never."
"Then why—"
I look around,
make sure no one else
can hear.
"I thought Santiago
would like it."
"Oh," says KeeLee,
sounding almost sad.
"What? You tried on heels," I say.
"But that was different,"
KeeLee says.
"That was for *me*,
not for someone else."
I don't want to listen
to what KeeLee has to say,
so I turn away and hurry
to the exit.

News Travels

Back home,
I rip the skirt off,
drop-kick it into
the back of the closet,
and pull on comfy jeans.
Later that night
when Dad gets home
in time for dinner,
he walks into the kitchen
all smiles,
checking me
from head to toe.
"So where is it?"
"Where's what?" I ask.
"The skirt?
Your mom told me
you bought one."
I groan so loudly
the whole world
can hear me,
then run to my room
and slam the door.
Before it closes,
my dad yells out,
"What did I say?"

Sick to My Stomach

I don't have a fever,
but it's not entirely a lie
when I tell my mom
I'm sick to my stomach
and need to stay home.
It hurts seeing Santiago
when he doesn't
see
me.

What Are Friends For?

KeeLee's a little mad at me
for giving her the slip
during fire drill.
Still, she drops by after choir
to check on the real reason
I'm feeling sick as a dog.
"Forget about Santiago," she says
when I tell her.
"He's probably not
good enough for you anyway."
"Probably not?"
"*Definitely* not."
KeeLee has a way
of making me smile.

Is Everybody Crazy Now?

Glory sits down to dinner
by invitation.
Jake does his usual drop-in
right when Mom sets the table.
I see him and cringe,
hoping he doesn't bring up Santiago.
I'm still trying to figure out a way
to get Santiago to like me.
"Great half-court shot
last Saturday," Dad says to Glory.
She smiles and we all rehash the game.
During cleanup,
Jake sneaks long looks at Glory
when her head is turned away.
"Man," Jake whispers,
"that girl's legs go on forever.
She seeing anybody?"
He's practically salivating.
I cut my eyes at him
and stomp off to the kitchen.
He's right behind me.
"Joy, what's the matter? What'd I say?"
"First, it's KeeLee. Now it's Glory.
It's okay if you're girl crazy, right?

But let me just *look* at Santiago
and you're all in my face."
"That's not true. I mean—
Look, it's different with you, okay?
I'm not trying to change myself for a girl.
But you're turning yourself
inside out for this guy,
and I don't see why.
There's nothing wrong with you
the way you are.
You don't need to become
somebody else."
I can't listen to this.
I drop a dish in the sink
and walk away.
"You don't like who I am now,"
I yell over my shoulder.
"Go find somebody you like better!"

Hiding Out

Shut up in my room for the night,
I jam on my headphones,
and crank the music up so high,
I don't have to think about why
I just told my best friend
to get lost.

Glee

Friday night,
the lights in the school auditorium
go dim.
A few weeks ago,
KeeLee told me I could invite Jake,
so he's there, three rows back.
We don't even wave to each other,
so I have no one to keep me company.
I sigh and silently wish KeeLee luck.
She looks so beautiful, so strong.
The lyrics of Christina Aguilera
fill the room.
"Words can't bring me down,"
sings KeeLee.
Her voice rubs the air
soft as silk
and I smile knowing
KeeLee doesn't need luck
after all.

The New Girl

I.
On Saturday,
I jog to the neighborhood
basketball court,
find Santiago
mixing it up
with some new girl.
A minute later,
their game is over
and they leave the court,
laughing at some private joke,
his arm slung across her shoulder
like he owns her.
I reel from the gut punch,
but can't keep from staring.
There's something about her,
something familiar.
The naked face,
unpainted lips,
plain hair flipped up
into a ponytail,
dirty sneaks,
boys' jogging shorts,

oversized shirt.
The new girl,
the old me—
we could be twins.

II.
I collapse
on the park bench,
wait till my heart stops
thundering inside my chest.
I feel something wet on my cheek,
wipe it away with the back of my hand,
and run all the way home.

Aftermath

Two days later,
I'm still mad.
Next team practice,
I snatch the ball
before my turn,
make a mad dash
for the hoop,
and slam the ball like
it's Santiago's face.
Coach doesn't even have to call time.
I bench myself
before he gets the chance.

Fuming

No point being mad
at Santiago.
He didn't tell me
to try to be
someone else.

Confession

Three days of moping
around the house,
and Mom is wondering why.
She bugs me
till I tell her about
Santiago,
the dumb things I did
to get his attention,
and the new girl
who didn't have to do
anything at all.
Mom listens, pushes the hair
from my forehead,
and asks me:
"Why do you care so much
whether he likes you?"
It's a hard question
and I take time to think
before I answer.
"Because—
because he makes
my heart beat fast."
"Oh, honey," Mom says,
"he may be the first,

but I promise you,
he won't be the last."
Then she holds me close
long enough for me to leave
a puddle on her shoulder,
long enough for me to feel
some of the hurt drain away.

The Call

One night
the phone rings.
Mom answers the call
then gives me the news
and the world falls away.
Some man was in his car
texting.
He never saw Jake
till it was too late.

S.O.S.

16 and ¼ blocks
from my house to
Columbia Presbyterian Hospital.
14 and ¼ blocks.
I run
counting each one.
12 and ¼ blocks.
Keeping count
gives me something
to concentrate on.
10 and ¼ blocks.
Something other than
my fear.
8 and ¼ blocks.
6 and ¼ blocks.
Oh, Lord.
Please!
3 and ¼ blocks.
I'm coming, Jake!
I'm coming!

Room 321

Room 321.
That's what the nurse told me.
The elevator groans
all the way up
to the third floor.
How long did I stand
outside his door,
afraid to go in,
afraid not to?
Why did I fight with him?
Jake is worth
ten Santiagos.
He's my friend.
What if Jake doesn't forgive me?
What if he doesn't wake up
long enough to try?
Hand shaking,
I grab the doorknob,
take a deep breath,
and push.

Vigil

Jake's mom
leaves us in the room alone.
I sit on the edge of his bed,
one hand holding his,
the other wiping
a stupid tear
from my cheek.
If I start bawling
like some little girl,
Jake will never let me
live it down.
I swallow hard
and give his hand a squeeze.
When he doesn't squeeze back
I die inside.
I lay my head down
on his blanket
and fight for breath.
When I can't stand
his stillness anymore,
I stumble out the door.

Concussion

Even the word sounds
like it could break you.
The doctor says
it's why Jake is still asleep.
But if the doctor's so smart,
how come he can't say
when my friend will wake up?
Or if?
I need an aspirin.

Visiting Hours Are Over

I take the stairs down
to the ground floor
so I can cry
in secret.
Once outside,
the cold air clears my mind.
I text KeeLee,
ask her to talk to God,
and to put in a good word
for Jake.

Gift

The next afternoon, I'm back
determined to get through to Jake.
I lean over his bed,
give him a shake.
"Enough already!"
I tell him.
"Wake up!"
That's when
Jake slowly opens his eyes
and gives me the shadow
of a grin.
It feels like Christmas.
"Hey," says Jake.
"Hey," I say,
and suddenly I know
this is all the conversation
I'm in the mood for.

Standing Watch

24 hours later,
I change my mind.
I want to hear more
than a word or two.
I want to see Jake move.
His stillness stops my heart.
Jake? Are you in there?

The Old Jake

Sitting up in bed,
laughing with his nurse,
the old Jake
sees me at the door,
fakes a shot
with an imaginary ball.
"Nothing but net!" he says,
then waves me in.
That's my Jake.
I can breathe again.

Peg-Leg

That's my new name for Jake.
Lucky for him
the driver wasn't going that fast
so the only thing broken
was his leg.
Still, he's pretty banged up.
But after watching Jake
for a few days,
the doctors
get him and his cast
up on crutches
and send him home.
That's good for me
'cause I'm worn out from running
back and forth
those 16 and ¼ blocks
to see him.

I Hate to Say It

I drop by Jake's after school,
find him in front of the television.
He makes a place for me
on the couch.
I grab the remote
mute the sound,
and get to the point:
"I'm sorry about our fight, Jake.
You were right."
The words are out
before I know it.
(What was it I said to Caden
about sticking with
who you really are?)
I tell Jake about
Santiago and the new girl,
and how ridiculous I feel.
"Don't call yourself ridiculous!"
Jake is quick to say.
"That's *my* job!"
It takes me a minute
to tell that he's joking,
to catch his grin.
But when I do,

I punch him in the arm,
smiling at my friend,
glad to have us back.

Readjustment

I sort through my closet
pack up the heels,
the skirt,
the lacy pink shirt I bought
when I was out of my mind.
And no more baggy pants.
I slip on a new pair of jeans
that hug.
They've got a few rhinestones
on the back pocket.
Nothing too girly.
Just a little.
Like me.

Guess Who's Coming to Dinner?

Mom makes a special dinner for Jake
once he gets good at
swinging himself around
on those crutches.
KeeLee comes over too.
She and Jake haven't seen each other
since he left the hospital.
KeeLee tells everyone about
the songs she's practicing
for the next show-choir concert.
Dad tells a few funny stories
about when he was in a band.
Caden asks Jake
a million questions about
how it feels to be hit by a car,
like it's some great adventure.
Then he asks if he can
draw something on Jake's cast.
Jake doesn't seem to mind.
Me, I'm quiet, for once,
taking it all in,
feeling like
I wouldn't trade places
with anyone.

ACKNOWLEDGMENTS

Storytelling is not a collaborative art, and yet there are always people in the life of the storyteller who help the story to be birthed.

Thanks to Bloomsbury for inviting me to write a poem for *First Kiss (Then Tell)*, the anthology that opened the door to this adventure.

Thanks to my faithful and sharp-eyed reader, Amy Malskeit, for offering valuable critiques from first draft to last.

Thanks to my editor, Victoria Wells Arms, for her patience.

Finally, thanks to the following ladies for generously sharing their stories of young love with me as inspiration: Barbara Bazaldua, Marie Bradby, Bev Gallagher, Becky Kirk, Candace Lazzaro, Tracy Roeder, Maria Salvadore, and Debra Jackson-Whyte.